George Anthony Denison

Mr. Gladstone

With an Appendix

George Anthony Denison

Mr. Gladstone
With an Appendix

ISBN/EAN: 9783744691819

Printed in Europe, USA, Canada, Australia, Japan

Cover: Foto ©Raphael Reischuk / pixelio.de

More available books at **www.hansebooks.com**

MR. GLADSTONE.

WITH APPENDIX,

CONTAINING THE

ACCUMULATED EVIDENCE

OF

FIFTY-FIVE YEARS.

A RETROSPECT AND PROSPECT.

WITH

SUMMARY

AND

NOTES.

Amici, Amici, sed Magis Amica Veritas.

Inscribed, in respect and love, to the

CLERGY AND PEOPLE

OF THE ARCHDEACONRY OF TAUNTON,

BY

GEORGE ANTHONY DENISON,

Vicar of East Brent, Archdeacon of Taunton.

LONDON:

WILLIAM RIDGWAY, 169, PICCADILLY, W.

1886.

1885.

To every Member of the Church of England.

WE GO FORTH,

NOT IN STRENGTH OR RIGHTEOUSNESS OF OUR OWN,

BUT

IN THE STRENGTH AND RIGHTEOUSNESS

OF

THE LORD GOD.

TO

FIGHT THE BATTLE

OF

THE CHURCH OF ENGLAND

AGAINST

THE LEADER OF "THE GREAT LIBERAL PARTY;"

THE AUTHOR OF

"THE CHURCH IN CONNECTION WITH THE STATE,"
1841.

BECAUSE THERE IS NONE OTHER
THAT FIGHTETH FOR US,
BUT ONLY THOU,

O GOD.

EAST BRENT,
December 11, 1885.

MR. GLADSTONE.

A RETROSPECT AND PROSPECT.

I DESIRE, first, to repeat here once more my great
regret for having, at an Election Meeting in
Somerset, November 5th, allowed myself to use
words in connection with Mr. Gladstone's name
which were, in themselves, and in their connection,
unfit, unseemly, and improper to be used, however
they may be explained and accounted for.

I took the first public opportunity at my command, the meeting for Defence of "Church and
State," held at Taunton, in the afternoon of
November 12th, the Bishop in the Chair, to
express this regret in words written down; and
would have repeated those words at the meeting
held the same evening in the same place, but was
refused a hearing.

Having said this, I return to my work of thirty-
four years—that is, to my unvarying public
opposition to Mr. Gladstone as Member of Parliament, and, most of all, as first Minister of the
Crown.

1

I have known Mr. Gladstone some fifty-five years. Being four years older than he is, I was not of his standing at Christ Church; but I knew him slightly then, and have had communication with him from time to time, more or less, before and since 1845.

I began to lose confidence in him as a politician in 1847, when it was with greatest difficulty that I was persuaded to vote for him at Oxford by my dear old friend Bishop Bagot.

In 1851 I lost all confidence in him.

In 1853 I did what I could to turn him out of Oxford; and, if my brethren clergy and laity had trusted me then, as I am thankful to believe they trust me now, should have turned him out.

In 1866, I did turn him out. Everybody knows well, who knows anything of the history of that election, that it was my action in London early in 1865 which issued, by natural consequence, in turning him out in 1866.*

Nothing has occurred since to lessen for one moment my distrust of Mr. Gladstone in respect of "Church and State." Distrust of him in this the chief particular of "English Policy," in the true sense of these words, as Member of Parliament, and, most of all, as first Minister of the Crown: but very much to keep it intact, alive, intent, and active.

On the other hand, I desire to say that I ha·

* "Notes of my Life." Third edition, pp. 334-8.

never doubted, and do not doubt, even now, that Mr. Gladstone who has, throughout his career, by the power of an intellect which has *no intuitions to guide it;** and is, therefore, free, in every separate case, to admit arguments on both sides, as, *à priori*, of equal value ; and who has from his boyhood, delighted in nothing so much as in; arraying upon every manner of topic—small or great, *pros* and *cons* —I say, I have never doubted that he has persuaded himself, in every instance, that he was only doing what it was his duty to do, in spite of arriving thereby—and this at very brief intervals of time— at positions and issues the most contradictory and mutually repugnant.

My quarrel, then, with him is not, and never has been, a personal quarrel in any sense. My contention is not against the man at all, who has so many claims to be honoured and loved, but against a habit of mind which makes him so entirely impossible to be depended upon as First Minister of the Crown, Minister of State, Member of Parliament—exponent and defender of the Constitution in " Church and State."

I have long been in possession of a most re- markable *catena* of evidence bearing directly upon the constitution of the mind of Mr. Gladstone, ᴼᴸnched. by his own admission to my dear friend ᵐristopher Wordsworth, late Bishop of Lincoln, Cᴵich I publish in Appendix.

See his own admission upon this point. (Appendix.) p. 38, note upon it, B.

I have shown it to many men, members of both Houses of Parliament, and others. Their remark upon it has always been that it has helped them to apprehend clearly and distinctly the character of the man, which before had puzzled them not a little.

Members of Parliament, more particularly of the House of Commons, who live day and night in the presence and in the fear of majority and minority, are sorely tempted to subject right or wrong in every manner of question to the test of majority or minority law, especially if they be Ministers of State: above all other, the First Minister is so tempted.

Mr. Gladstone is a memorable example of the extent to which this disease—and it is a very bad disease—may be upon the brain.

When he began his public life, some forty-five years ago, he never so much as dreamt of saying, or suggesting even, which is more in his line, that it was "an open question" whether or no it would be a sufficient warrant for taking in hand what is vulgarly called "dis-Establishment" and "dis-Endowment"—two things not separable the one from the other—that a majority of the people of England should demand them at the hands of the "Governing Power."

But the long habit of governing, and his belief that he is the only man who can govern England*

* See Appendix of Evidence, p. 39.

has been too much for him even upon such a question as this, which, in the nature of the thing, is not subject to majority and minority law; and which, therefore, *may not* at any time be brought in England within the category of " practical politics."

I should have said "in Ireland" too ; only that the thing is already done, leaving its precedent for the *civil* marriage of " dis-Establishment " with " dis-Endowment," and yet more for the " robbery of GOD" in tithes and offerings, which is inherent in every application of Church property to secular uses.

Mr. Gladstone, in common with other " Liberals," and lately he has got into very bad company—the worst, indeed, I think, that he could find—has fallen, all his logic and rhetoric notwithstanding, into the fallacy of confounding things in their nature and properties things distinct. For example, there is the application of the majority law by right reason, and there is an application of the same law by wrong, force, tyranny, robbery.

It would appear that at the close of his public life he has arrived at the preposterous fallacy of making these two into one, with view to the tricking out and colouring of the last. And when a man of his high and commanding position, power of speech, and peculiar talent of mystifying other men, takes a thing of this kind in hand, he succeeds to an extent which leaves only a very poor opinion of the reasoning faculty, depth, and clearness of knowledge of men and things in those who, in the jargon of the day, and after the fashion of the close of Century XIX, are called "Educated People," "People of Culture."

Mr. Gladstone, by his failing to observe and insist upon the distinction between application of majority law by right reason, and of the same law by wrong, force, tyranny, robbery, has been justly claimed by the force party.

He makes a feeble, and, if the subject-matter were not so grave, a laughable, attempt to escape from the grasp of the force party. He says, "There is a good deal to be said on your side; and if you can show a majority, it is very cogent. But, if you please, just at present, it is not convenient for the purposes and cohesion of 'the great Liberal party' to make a point of it, as part of our Manifesto."

It will be seen from the Appendix* that Mr. Gladstone's habit of subjecting every manner of question to the array of "*pros*" and "*cons*" began with his early boyhood, and has prevailed all along. How this came to be so will also be seen there from his own admission. No doubt the fact shows a principal misfortune in the history of any man's life; and however its consequences may not declare themselves in boyhood or early manhood, as is very true in Mr. Gladstone's case, they are quite certain to declare themselves in later years; more

* Appendix, p. 37.

particularly are they sure to do this in the case of a man like him who has lived *for* and *to* "govern England."

A Christian statesman may have, in his own person, and as representing others, to suffer heavily under the application of majority law by the force which confounds things sacred, and so outside the province of human arbitrament, with things within it. But to give way to force which you cannot overcome, is one thing, and to be an initiating, or in any measure or manner a consenting party to it, is another thing.

It is surely not for nothing that S. Paul, writing to Timothy, his " own son in the faith," says of the power of early training and consequent intuition, " When I call to remembrance the unfeigned faith that is in thee, which dwelt first in thy grandmother Lois, and thy mother Eunice, and I am persuaded that in thee also."*

The influences of place, power; most of all, party, are corrupting influences.

It is a very melancholy history of a great life. With all his high character, transcendent ability, largest application of it to subjects of every class, Mr. Gladstone has done more to lower and injure political morality than any man of his time.

Amici, Amici ;
Sed magis Amica
Veritas.

* 1 Timothy i. 2 . 2 Timothy i. 5.

There is another matter—the manner of the late extension of the Franchise—which cannot be passed over.

"The great Liberal party" being in great straits—weakened very seriously in Parliament by gross and unpardonable mismanagement of chief interests of England, especially in Northern and Southern Africa, by the heartless and unblushing sacrifice of Gordon, by blundering playing into the hands of Russia on confines of our Indian Empire; by an unprecedentedly reckless expenditure; above all, by schism in the Cabinet, coming of the importation of Messrs. Chamberlain and Dilke—the great Liberal party, with "the Nonconformist its backbone,' cast about how to reinforce their numbers in the House of Commons, and to deal severely with the House of Lords.

Extension of the Franchise to a class of men notoriously not possessed of the knowledge qualifying to exercise it as it requires to be exercised; and, in their natural want of sufficient information, open, especially in the country parishes, to bribery and corruption of the most ridiculous and contemptible description—houses, lands, horses, cows, sheep, pigs, all for nothing; this was the over-clever device of the framer of the late "Reform" Act—the *Via prima Salutis*.

Now,—to take the low ground—let it be supposed for a moment that these very questionable means resorted to to gain votes or the "great

Liberal party" meet with some "success"—everybody knows, elector and non-elector, that the two
millions will have found out long before the next
Election all the trick of the new "Reform" Bill—
will be somewhat angry at getting nothing but
words; will not be overpleased with the compliment
paid to their understanding; and if they trouble
themselves to exercise their franchise again, will
not exercise it on the "Liberal" side.*

I will add here something about politics generally. It is, comparatively, of no importance in
itself, but it may help to clear men's minds upon
present prospects.

I am an old Tory. I never liked a Whig as a
Whig. I could not. I have had, and have kindest,
nearest, and dearest personal friends, connections
among Whigs ; but, as Whigs, I have never liked
them. I am not fond of a Conservative either,
as a Conservative. The Tory is the one true
Defender, Reformer and Promoter.

The Whigs have been playing so long with the
edge tools of Mr. Gladstone and his Red Radical
friends that they have cut their fingers and maimed
their thumbs, and cannot nip anything tight. The
Conservatives have been playing ever since 1832
with the same tools, handed over to them by the
Whigs. The only difference is that the Conservative has blunted the tools a little, so that they
don't cut sharply, but clumsily and painfully—

* The new Parliament will go down in our history as
"The Cow and Acre Parliament." So also *now* the new
Government, February, 1886.—Note C.

2

crush and bruise rather than cut. I have a great many very dear Conservative friends, but, as Conservatives, I don't love them much. (Note E.)

Then there is the Red Radical—Birmingham Caucus, represented by Messrs. Chamberlain and Dilke—I need say no word about them. Nevertheless, I admit that, unwittingly, they have done Churchmen very good service. They have waked Churchmen up; by no means an easy thing to do; as I know very well by much painful personal experience, extending over many years.

For "Liberal Conservatives" and "Conservative Liberals," I have no conception what the terms mean.

Lastly, there is "the Opportunist." Mr. Gladstone is the Prince of "Opportunists;" watching and waiting for every opportunity of adding to the strength of "the Great Liberal Party" in House of Commons, whatever be the nature, character, occasion of the opportunity.

If any number of Bradlaughs present themselves *to take the Oath,* Mr. Gladstone, having written over the door of the House of Commons,

"Civil and Irreligious Liberty,"

is bound to be the first to open the door, to usher and welcome in.

Are they not an important section of "the Great Liberal Party"?

Mr. Gladstone again is not satisfied with paving the way by present deprecation, for severance of State from Church *in another Parliament.*

He fills up the interval with such things as "marriage with a deceased wife's sister," a thing in itself, and in its necessary adjuncts and followings, the breaking up by Law of the Land of all sanctity and purity of Marriage.

Mr. Gladstone, the nominal leader of "the great Liberal Party," says to frightened Whigs for their consolation, and to Red Radicals for their encouragement—in Manifesto espousing both sides of the question, *more suo*—"Hold hard—I'm not ready! Not 'just at present.' Your time will come—don't be in such a hurry, or you will dislocate, and break into little bits 'the great Liberal party' —of which, as I have told you before, 'the Nonconformist is the backbone.' Take your time. It is 'an open question.'" Mr. Gladstone is the Prince of Opportunists. Now, an "Opportunist" means a man who is intent, *above all other things*, upon carrying out his "opportunity." This is his mania ; he will sacrifice everything else to compass it—whether the thing he wants opportunity for be good or bad for his country. This comes in, if at all, as the second and inferior consideration.

He wants something for his party ; that is, for "the great Liberal party "—for an "Opportunist " is always a "Liberal,"—and watches his opportunity. If this comes suddenly, it sweeps him along without allowing him a moment to pause and consider what it is he is about. For Opportunism possesses this inherent power of making its disciple sacrifice everything to the joy of a *coup d'état.*

Mr. Gladstone's memorable action in the matter of what is vulgarly called " Irish dis-Establishment " is an instance in point. In 1865 he wrote : " it was a subject he need not go into because it was "not within the range of practical politics." When Lord Mayo proposed in 1868 what was called "levelling up," Mr. Gladstone, two years and six months after what he wrote in 1865, saw his opportunity and proposed and carried "levelling down." It may very well be that a like revolutionary assault is near at hand, however disclaimed, for the Church of England; so soon, that is, as the "opportunity" comes, if Mr. Gladstone returns to power.

The late Lord Derby—once a Whig—said, when he proposed his Reform Bill, " We have dished the Whigs." He anticipated a little—claimed all too soon. He has left it to Mr. Gladstone to *dish up* the Whigs—that is, to leave them the choice of becoming "Opportunists" with himself, as described above. or of joining loyally hand-in-hand with those whose business it is, under God, to save the old Constitution in " Church and State." And so with these contingencies before me, I thank Messrs. Chamberlain and Dilke, and have some kindly feeling towards the Birmingham Caucus, for waking up Churchmen to "contend earnestly" for "Church and State." But I cannot thank the man who, assuring me that he cares much for me and mine, is only biding his time, and watching and waiting for his " opportunity " to destroy me more easily than he can do "just at present."

It is proposed on the part of the Birmingham Caucus, represented by Messrs Chamberlain and Dilke, some few years ago imported into the Cabinet by Mr. Gladstone, to sever finally and absolutely—not bit by bit only, as has been done in so many principal instances since 1832—but finally and absolutely *en masse*—once for all, the State of England from the Church of England—that is, to make the Church *of* England cease and determine; and to leave the Church *in* England disinherited and robbed by man, to begin anew after a life of some one thousand five hundred years; and, so far as the English nation is concerned, to take its only recognized status and position among the Sects.

Now, the Church Catholic, The Church of the Incarnation, The Church of the Cross, The Church of the Resurrection, The Church of the Ascension, The Church of Pentecost, The Church of the Orders, The Creeds, The Sacraments, is the One place of " The Truth;" the One place of " Salvation" in Life, in Death, in Judgment, vouchsafed of GOD to the World in and by His Holy Word, for JESUS CHRIST'S sake.

To the Bishops, Clergy, People of England, " The Church of England," and none other, is " The

14

Church Catholic." To live in, by, for " The Church of England " is the highest happiness of the Englishman, woman, child.

Wherefore, to discredit, dishonour, rob " The Church of England " is the worst national sin that the Governing Power of England can commit; and therein and thereby invite the People of England to commit in its train. Further, it is the surest way to the persuading the People of England to "tempt GOD "* in and by doubting Him and His Truth; and step by step to become an Infidel People. It does this by taking away from before their eyes, from before the heart and mind of their daily life, The Authority Divine; and by bringing into its place the deadly fruit of the " Pride of Life,"† the countless inventions and contradictions of men ; inventing a human salvation, and devising in almost every conceivable shape a new Providence.

For Mr. Chamberlain and the Birmingham Caucus, and for Mr. Gladstone's connection with both, I have then this to say—

Is there not a cause, more than a cause, for distrust, aye for condemnation of the "practical Politics," which, for the sake of Mr. Chamberlain with his following, have invited‡ into the inner

* Thou shalt not tempt The LORD thy GOD.—Deut. vi. 16.; St. Luke iv. 12.

† 1 St. John ii. 16.　　　　‡ 2 St. John, 10.

Councils of The Crown, The Unitarian Non-Conformist, The denier of THE ETERNAL SON? The man who says—" I am rich and increased with "goods and have need of nothing, and knoweth " not that he is miserable and poor and blind " and naked."—Revelation iii. 17.

On the other hand, is there not a cause, more than a cause, for rejoicing and thankfulness that, although it be not for the sake of The Church of England, nor for the sake of Members of The Church of England, yet that it is for Religion's sake, in the foresight of the sure deep and lasting injury to Religion in Europe, and in many other parts of the World, that very eminent men in The Church of Rome, both in and out of England should have lifted up their voice before The World to denounce all and every attempt to sever The State of England from the Church of England?

Unwittingly, indeed, and in the moral blindness which *always* accompanies un-Belief in The Incarnation, Mr. Chamberlain has done us Church People of the Church of England very good service.

If Parliament violates, and therein lowers "the Church," the One appointed witness to the One Truth of God, to a thing of man's invention, in the eyes of the people, it does all that can be done by man to make the people say with Pilate, " What is Truth?" In other words, to make the people of England first a doubting, then a disbelieving, finally an apostate people.

I have endeavoured to put this matter upon its first principles. It is not a matter which ought to be argued upon subordinate ground or upon inferior issue. The subjoined Resolutions convey my meaning :—

RESOLUTIONS.

1. That to sever the State of England from the Church of England cannot be done without sin; inasmuch as it is to reject by the National voice the first and greatest gift of GOD to the people of England.

2. That the removal of the Bishops from the House of Lords is an integral part of such severance, being the destruction of one of the four elements of the Constitution in Church and State —(1) The Crown, the Defender of the Faith; (2) The Lords Spiritual; (3) The Lords Temporal; (4) The Commons. That such removal is therefore not within the province of Constitutional Legislation.

3. That to apply any portion of the present or future endowment of the Church of England to secular use is to " rob GOD."

Of all attempts to rob by Act of Parliament—I do not say *a fortiori* by a Parliament of all religions and of none, for the constitution of Parliament makes no real difference in the thing done— there is no attempt so bad in all its aspects, in itself, and in every one of its effects and issues,

public and private, as the attempt to rob the people
of England of

The Church

of

England.

I do not say of

The Church

in

England.

For this is a thing not within the power of any
number of Parliaments, whether they be Parliaments of (so-called) Churchmen, or Parliaments
like the present, of men of all religions and of none.

On the other hand, Parliament can rob the people
of England of

The Church

of

England.

And in so doing commit the greatest sin in the
power of Parliament to commit. For, whether
" Church *of* England " or " Church *in* England,"
both are Gifts of GOD to this People, and to sin
against one is to sin against the other; the only
difference being that in the one case the sin can
take effect, and in the other it cannot.

First, then, a few words touching

The Church

in

England.

That is, the Church planted here before England

was a People; the Church which has seen the State of England grow up around her; the Church the vital principle of all the after-life of England.

If the Church in England be dated only from S. Augustine, 597 A.D. (which is to make a very large admission indeed, but may be made here for convenience sake), the Parliament of England dates from A.D. 1295. "The Church" both "*in* England" and "*of* England" is 700 years before the Parliaments of England. The Church of England, upon the data here allowed, is close upon 1300 years old; the Parliaments of England close upon 600 years old.

Now, The World says Parliament can do everything.

"Let the dead bury their dead."   S. Matt. viii. 22.

There is at least one thing the Parliament of England cannot do, and that is to rob the people of England of the Church

in

England.

For to remove a "Church" is a thing belonging to Visitation of GOD only—Visitation of GOD upon the faithlessness of the baptized: faithlessness accumulated in its several kinds for shorter or longer time, and finally culminating at that point which calls down, first, the warnings, then the threatenings, then the wrath of GOD, scattering His Church, wheresoever planted, to the four winds of Heaven.

Chapters II and III of "The Revelation" set

forth examples both of Churches faithful in suffering manifold, and of Churches guilty of unfaithfulness; with warning and threatening to these of the final Consummation of the Wrath of GOD. The Church *in* England can never die so long as it be not finally found of GOD to be unfaithful.

Let me note here that the word "Church" means the Body of the Baptized, possessing by Gift of GOD, the Orders, the Creeds, the Sacraments, as derived by It from Command and Institution of CHRIST as recorded in Holy Scripture under the promised guidance of the Spirit of Truth, the Comforter. This Church in the Providence of GOD has become "The Church *of* England." "The Church of England" is, to the People of England, "The Church Catholic."

There is one other note to be added here.

I put it by way of question and answer.

Q.—What is Holy Scripture?

A.—It is the Canonical Books of the Old and the New Testaments. Article VI.

Q.—What is "Canonical?"

A.—"Canonical" from κανών Canon-Rule.

In respect of Holy Scripture, "Canonical" is that which being "commonly received"—Article VI—in the Church under guidance of GOD the Holy Ghost, is finally, under the same guidance, ruled and sealed for the Church Catholic and for

3 *

the whole world, in His own good time, by Council of the Church Catholic.

The Canon or Rule of Holy Scripture was first so ruled by the Council of Laodicea, Cent. IV.

The Canons of this Council were afterwards received into the Code of the Canons of the Church Universal.

"The Revelation" is not found in the catalogue of Canonical books in Canon of Council of Laodicea.

The account of this omission is variously stated.

But it is not disputed that the Book of The Revelation, as we have it, has been "commonly received" in the Church as of Authority Divine both before and after the Council.

Further, that for us, for every one of us, Bishops, Clergy, People of the Church of England, it is, in common with all the other books of the New Testament, humbly and thankfully accepted as Canonical, and made part of the use of the Church of England.

The conclusion is one from which there is no escape.

That conclusion is, that the Church is *the one* channel and instrument by and through which, in the Providence of GOD, it has been given to all men *to know of a certainty* what *is* Holy Scripture and what *is not*.

Now I believe that this great fact of the Christian dispensation is one very commonly, so to speak, *unknown* to those who are not of the Church; or, at least, not plainly placed before them. I believe further that it is not commonly insisted upon by Churchmen themselves among the chief grounds for "Authority of the Church in controversies of Faith." Article XX. For that which has been made in the Providence of God witness and keeper of Holy Writ is also interpreter of Holy Writ.

It may therefore be good to call close attention to the account of how it is that we all, Church people and not Church people alike, *know of a certainty*, not of human origin but of Divine, that " The Bible " *is* " The Bible," *i.e.*, The Book of GOD.

Men of "all denominations" are continually appealing to the Bible as against the Church. Well, it ought at least to make them pause and consider a little that it is " The Church " only which has, under GOD, given them the Bible to appeal to ; and especially at such times as these times of ours, when they are tempted to cry " Down with the Church " : " Down with it, even to the ground."

I turn now to the Church
of
England.

How did the Church *in* England become the Church of England ? The answer is one and one only—By Gift of GOD.

The seed sown here very early in the history of

the Church of CHRIST grew and became a great Tree, so that men, governors and people "come and lodge under the branches of it" (St. Matt. xiii. 32).

It is the Church of "the Constitutions of Clarendon," providing for equal justice in spiritual and civil causes.   Henry II, A.D. 1164.

It is the Church of the Barons of England. The Church of "Magna Charta," affirming the true liberty of the Church of England as against the Church of Rome, "*Libera sit Ecclesia Anglicana*," King John, A.D. 1215.   Observe it is *Ecclesia Anglicana*—not *Ecclesia Romana*.

It is again the Church of the Barons of England, Henry III, A.D. 1272, refusing to accommodate the Common law of England to the Canon Law in respect of children not born in wedlock.

"*Nolumus Leges Angliæ mutari.*"

"We will not have the laws of England touched."

Observe that the latest of these instances of the jealous guardianship of the then Governing Powers of England over the true position, interests and liberties of the Church of England is 23 years before the birth of Parliament.

Now the common language of our days speaks of the Church as "established," "established by law," "as by law established," and we hear the Church spoken of as "the establishment." The modern purpose in so speaking of It being to create in the popular mind—which, in proportion to its necessary ignorance, is regarded by " the great Liberal party" as the most promising field in which to work—the belief that it is a Church made by man's law; and, therefore, justly liable to be dealt with in all its life and substance by man's law.

It is a vulgar error ; but so common and so employed for worst uses as to demand correcting and exposing.

" Dolus latet in generalibus."

There are then *three* senses in which the words " establishing," " established by law," " as by law established," are applied to " the Church."

1. The sense of the adversaries of " the Church," *i.e.*, the sense of *creating by man's act.*
2. The sense of establishing by man's faithful recognition of what exists *à priori* by Gift of GOD.
3. The sense of establishing by man's humble acceptance of such existence as the greatest Gift of GOD to a People.

1. is absolutely, not only untrue, but impossible —a people cannot create a Church any more than a man can, not being specially commissioned thereto by GOD ; though it be not an uncommon error, one with which the world is every day more and more familiar, that a man can.

2. and 3. are true. The State of England could not help, if it had wished it, recognizing the fact of the prior existence of the Church of England. Nor again could the State of England do other

than accept the Church of England given of God, and endowed by the *private* almsgiving of His People in Christ, for the Ministry and Service of God, and the better care of His Poor, as the National Church, by its Common and Statute Law.

And so we sweep away the cobwebs about "establishment," and never use, except for convenience and under protest, the words "established," "dis-Established." They find no proper place in this matter, any more than "endowed," "dis-Endowed," which imply about as big an untruth as can anywhere be found. Namely, that the Church of England has been endowed by the Civil Power of England, and that, *therefore*, the Civil Power may justly dis-Endow.

When I have to speak or write in this matter, instead of using "dis-Establishment," I use "severing the State of England from the Church of England;" and I call it—what it is—a sin; and instead of dis-Endowing, I use "robbing God," which are the only two words which describe the truth of the case. See Resolutions cited above.

Of all signs of and grounds for fear of what is coming; has come in its beginnings, and in all its ever-growing and accumulating power for evil upon this People, there is no one to compare with the "Board School."

It is the proclamation by the public voice—

That secular instruction is a necessity for a

Christian people, but that religious Education is not.

The Board School tramples upon the special plea of the religious conscience of the parent as conveyed in and by the original Conscience Clause, employed, down to 1870, as the lever whereby the Church School was upheaved from its foundations, and which had *betrayed* the Church School into a position *contrary to* its inherent nature and office.

The plea, having thus done its insidious work, was cast aside for a thing its precise contradictory.

The method and manner of this thing was the making the secular education of the child *compulsory upon the parent by way of fine, all his religious conscience notwithstanding.*

Thus the " religious Conscience " of the parent, refusing to send his child to a school where religious teaching is set aside, is converted from its former highly vaunted and patronized position into a foolishness on the parent's part, to be visited by compulsion in the shape of fine.

For the child, the Board School has provided a place for the sure daily growth of neglect of prayer to GOD for JESUS' sake; with a like neglect of the means of daily hearing of and instruction in the Holy Scriptures. That is to say, a place for the sure daily growth of Indifferentism, the parent of Infidelity. The Creation of the Board School is the despising and the selling of the " Birthright." (See

4

Note D.) It is a National Act which has " no place of repentance."

Now it would be wonderful, if fear did not cast wonder out, to see the general content ; nay, the approval; nay, the satisfaction; nay, the complacency of Churchmen very generally, Bishops, priests, people, with the Act for " Elementary Education," A.D. 1870; with all its flimsy and fraudulent pretence of justice to the Church by way of the " Time table Conscience Clause," which robs the Parish Priest of his office, and turns the *Religious training* of the Children of the Church into one of the lessons of the school, having, as they have, its own half-hour, and no more.

Men's eyes are opening fast now ; aye, but under what power? The power of a shilling rate.

The Act of 1870 was the Act of a Government of which Mr. Gladstone was first Minister.

I turn back to letters, down to some twenty-three years before 1870, to lay my hands upon the proof that Mr. Gladstone would then no more than I would myself *then* and *now*, have lifted his little finger to help the Act of 1870.

What remains to complete the policy of "the great Liberal party," to seal with its seal the "presumptuous sin," the "great offence?"

Dis-Establish and dis-Endow "the Church of England."

Fiat Ruina, ruat Cœlum. Disinherit the Church as you have disinherited the Church School. Make the path of Indifferentism and Infidelity plain before every face.

Have no care remaining for Ordination vow; for Office, and Commission of the parish priest. Have no care for the poor and the not poor alike of the Church of CHRIST.

These are "practical politics" of "the great Liberal party."

The "great Liberal party" are forgetting fast, if they ever knew it, that, as the School is, so will be the People. An irreligious School has the curse upon it of bequeathing from generation to generation a more and more irreligious People.

For some years past "the great Liberal party" have shown many signs that their main purpose is to do away with the Church of England.

The purpose is now definitely avowed, and made an election cry.

Mr. Gladstone is nominally the leader; is really a follower only in the wake of the true leader of "the great Liberal party."

I have never been able to think of Mr. Gladstone as a statesman. A statesman does not live from hand to mouth. Mr. Gladstone has lived from hand to mouth all along. A statesman is not an "Opportunist." Mr. Gladstone is the Prince of

" Opportunists." A Christian statesman does not range *all* questions of whatever character under the category of " practical politics." Mr. Gladstone does. This is, I believe, inseparable from the constitution and habit of his mind. His power of speaking no man can dispute any more than the marvellous range of his knowledge. But there are two kinds of this power—one good, the other not. The first is that which explains lucidly and beautifully, bases upon recognized principles, clears step by step, and so leaves a definite impression on the public mind and a guarantee of corresponding action. The other is that which, I may say, abuses itself, in abusing its own power; that which subtilizes, refines, mystifies, clouds, and leaves the hearer with the unpleasant feeling that he has heard something *very fine*, but *why fine* he cannot tell.

It is curious to note how in his downward progress towards Democracy, Mr. Gladstone has assumed that *the test* of the claim of a Church to be preserved intact, untouched by "convenient" Acts of Parliament, and not robbed by the State of what the State has not given one farthing of, is whether it is the Church of *the majority of the people*. It is a very curious test for a Christian man to apply. It smells strongly of the Birmingham Caucus, Messrs. Chamberlain and Dilke.

But this is not all. The money and lands of

the Church so robbed by the State—what is called
" the surplus of it "—is applied to all manner of
secular uses; to relieve ratepayers, &c.

This is the Irish case. Will the People of
England not be warned even yet? Dishonour to
GOD, and robbery of tithes and offerings, are pre-
cedents as astounding as they are evil, especially
in a Churchman's hands.

There is about it all a " *Cacoethes Spoliandi*," a
very strong Democratic dose.

It was wittily said by a member of House of
Commons not long ago—" As for time of House
of Commons, half of it is spent in listening to
Mr. Gladstone, and the other half in trying to find
out what he means, without succeeding in the
attempt." I don't, then, call Mr. Gladstone a
statesman, nor, with all his power of words and
word-painting, do I call him an orator. And even
if he be an orator, it is well cited from Grote, in
one of the ablest productions of this day, that
" Plato has ranked the rhetor in the same category
as the despot." *

England is fast finding Mr. Gladstone out. He
is not the power he was. That has been gone some
time. It is not easy to find words to say how
justly, but I say more, I believe him to be about
to cease to be a power at all.

* "Mr. Gladstone, or Gorgias the Rhetor." Bradbury,
Agnew, & Co., Whitefriars.

The English people, with all their self-confidence taken into account, find it, after all, a necessity to have something *outside themselves* upon which to rest. This cannot be taken to be found, except under the temporary delusion coming of fine words, in a man who has nothing really to give but words only, nothing to show but perpetual contradictions and perpetual failures—sometimes, alas, as in the terrible Gordon case, without honour wherewith to make at least some compensation.

In sum, I am compelled to say that the experience of a long life, with very uncommon means of forming a close and accurate judgment, does not supply me with a more melancholy history than that of Mr. Gladstone's public career. I say his public career. Of his private career I have not intimate knowledge: but he must be a despicable public adversary who does not speak all his mind in admiration and honour of that in which he knows no flaw.

For myself, let me say this much. Born and baptized in the Church of England, I have never for one moment—even in time of severest distress of mind by reason of dishonour and injury and robbery done many times during the last fifty years by the Civil Power to the Church of England—known, nor been able to understand the temptations to desert the Church of England.

Where I was born and baptized, by the mercy of God, I hope to die.

My Belief has always been in substance what it is now. It would be absurd to say that it has not been enlarged and intensified—I am a "High Churchman." Perhaps there is no man in England a higher Churchman. But then it has been all along, and is, the High Churchmanship of the Church of England *only*. I have never had yearnings for any other "High Churchmanship." I have the Orders, the Creeds, the Sacraments. I have the Bible to teach, the Prayer Book to guide me. I am where the Providence of God has placed me—what more do I want? All I want is to strive more to live up to the Rule *given me*. I may not invent for myself another Rule, nor devise another Providence.

I am said to be a "Ritualist," it is made a reproach to me. I know what the reproach means. It means I am a concealed and traitorous Roman Catholic.

Now my "Ritualism" is this—

1. I have had Matins and Evensong daily in my church for more than forty years.

2. I have had Daily Celebration of the Blessed Sacrament more than twelve years.

3. I stand at the Altar facing the East.

4. I celebrate always with Lights upon the Altar.

5. I kneel with the congregation at the words, "Who for us men and for our Salvation came

" down from Heaven, and was incarnate by THE
" HOLY GHOST of the Virgin Mary, and was made
" man."

6. I wear the surplice and coloured stole,
marking days and seasons in the Church's order.

7. I bow to the Altar, and cross myself frequently.

I am charged with having changed my
" opinions "—those poor things called " opinions "
—and therefore with being not worthy of credit. I
have heartily repented of such changes, and have
many times confessed this publicly, and have
returned to a better mind. There were three cases.
One was a change of " opinion " Civil. The other
two " of opinion " Ecclesiastical. I· cannot be far
from the close of a long life, and cannot contemplate
any other change. My Belief and my desire to be
always faithful to the Church of England has
never changed.

In 1832, for six months, I was in favour of the
Reform of the House of Commons. At the end of
the six months I came to my senses.

In 1851, under the very grievous burden of the
Gorham Judgment—without meaning " dis-Establishment " at all, I wrote " why should the Bishops
continue to sit in the House of Lords ?" which
implies " dis-Establishment." I have come to my
senses again here, both generally and particularly.

Lastly,—and this is the worst—being deeply

distressed by the many inroads made by the Civil Power upon the position of " The Church of England " since 1832, I did for some years, join myself to those who are for what is vulgarly called "dis-Establishment." I don't think much was said by promoters of the movement about its *twin-sister*," " dis-Endowment." I have, for a good many years now, seen all my unwisdom here also, and, as in other cases, have returned to my senses, and confessed my fault.

When Oxford University, with its motto " *Dominus Illuminatio Mea*," paraded still, became *corporately* a place of irreligion, and not even nominally a place of " Education of the Christian man," but of secular instruction only, I took my name off the books.

I keep in heart and mind the great words of Bishop Ken, in his Will—

" As for my Religion, I die in the Holy Catholic and Apostolical Faith professed by the whole Church before the disunion of East and West : more particularly, I die in the Communion of the Church of England, as it stands distinguished from all Papal and Puritan innovation, and as it adheres to the Doctrine of the Cross."

APPENDIX.

Habit of mind of Mr. Gladstone. Accumulated Evidence thereupon of 55 years, clenched by his own admission.

I LEFT Eton, Christmas, 1819, some four years, I think, before Mr. Gladstone went to Eton. In January, 1824, my two brothers, Henry and Stephen Charles Denison, went to Eton. Stephen, the younger of the two, became a very near friend of Mr. Gladstone, and, as will appear in the sequel of this paper, knew all about him.

When in 1828 I went from Christ Church as Fellow of Oriel, one of the nearest and dearest friends I have had was Augustus Page Saunders, then Curate to the Bishop of Oxford at Cuddesdon, and Mathematical Tutor at Christ Church; afterwards Head Master of Charter House, and finally Dean of Peterborough.

Of all the men I have known very intimately, he was the man of the largest intuitive power in respect of apprehending character and habit of mind in other men.

He was also a great scholar and mathematician, and naturally attracted to himself very many, I think nearly all, of those young men then passing through their life at Christ Church to highest honours in the schools—and all but one into high office in Church and State. Some names I recall—John Chetwynd Talbot, the Bruces Walter Hamilton, afterwards Bishop of Salisbury, C. Canning, C. Wordsworth, Bishop of St. Andrews, my brother Henry, W. E. Gladstone.

I used to come frequently to Saunder's rooms from Oriel in the evening.

One night in November, 1832, I was there talking over his pupils. He hit them off one after the other in a way, as proved by after years' experience, very wonderful.

At last we came to Gladstone, who had just got his double first class—a man of unblemished character, great scholar, showing high promise of oratorical power, said to be going into public life. Many eyes and minds were fixed upon him.

I said to Saunders, "Now, old man, there is one left I want to know something about, Gladstone ; and then I'll go to bed, for I shall have had from you as much to digest as will serve me for some time about all these men."

He said "I'll tell you about Gladstone in a minute." I said "What is it, then ? " He said, "*His conscience is so tender he will never go straight.*"

I heard, and wondered. At first I could not take it in. It is now fifty-three years ago. I learnt by degrees to apprehend by manifold experiences all that the words meant.

I kept applying the words, as time went on, to Gladstone's public career for some thirty years. In the course of those years I had a good deal of communication with him upon various matters of deep interest. The School Controversy, the Divorce Legislation, and, I think, Church Rates, with other things of deep public interest coming up from time to time.

I had found invariably that there was no bringing him to decisions. His leaning then—at least for the early part of the time—was the same way as my own. But my mind was definitely made up upon each and every point. He gave me the impression that he was always debating with himself, and never concluding for maintaining, but for sacrificing, in one shape or another.

In 1847 this presented itself to me so strongly that it was with the utmost difficulty that I was persuaded by my dear old friend, Bishop Bagot, to vote for him at Oxford. In 1851 I found I could no longer place any confidence in him. In 1853 I did what I could to turn him out of Oxford.

From January, 1854, to February, 1858, my time and energies were taken up by the prosecution against me touching the "Real Presence." In 1856, after the Bath Judgment, Mr. Gladstone most kindly and forgivingly asked me to come to Hawarden with my dear brother Robert Phillimore, to consult about best manner of defence. I was there some days, and at one time thought that I would adopt the plan of defence suggested to me. But soon after returned to my own mind upon it.

Somewhere about 1860 I was talking with my neighbour and friend Lake, now Dean of Durham, chairman of Gladstone's Committee at Oxford, and rector of Huntspill, not far from East Brent.

I had not mentioned Gladstone's name to him. I never did, because naturally I felt sure we should not agree.

All on a sudden he said, "*I say, Denison, I think I must give up Gladstone.*"

I said, "What ' *Et Tu Brute* '—mind, I did not begin this, but as you have begun it, may I ask why?"

He said "*I think his intellect can persuade his conscience of anything.*"

"Dear me," I said to myself, "that is what Saunders had prospectively in his mind when he said, ' *His conscience is so tender, he will never go straight.*' He was speaking of the boy and his young mind before it got into the struggle, and conflicting influences of public life. Lake is speaking of the public man so well known. So changed from his early political and ecclesiastical belief. So uncertain as I have found him myself. How curious it all is. I must know more about it."

So I sent Saunder's words and Lake's to my brother Stephen.

He wrote back :

" Very good stories and very true; but not all the Truth."

I asked, " What is all the truth ?"—He wrote—" *He* (Gladstone) *never had a conscience.*"

" Well," I replied, " My dear Stephen, this is strange enough, you nearly quarrelled with me for trying to turn out Gladstone, you subscribed largely to his fund; and now you tell me he never had a conscience.

" Oh," he said, " Don't misapprehend me. I am saying nothing against his moral character."

" Ah," said I, " When a man says of another, ' he never had a conscience,' it is commonly thought that he is saying something that way."

" No," he replied, " I mean nothing of the kind; what I mean is that *he never had so much as one intuition to begin with.* I have known him very well, nobody better, and I say that in every matter, little or big, which his mind rests upon, he is always marshalling the *pros* and the *cons* and building up conclusions *which he is just as likely as not to pull down the next or the same day.*"

Not long after this, I was, coming down by G.W.R., with my dear friend the late Bishop of Lincoln, Christopher Wordsworth. Something brought up Gladstone. We were alone in the carriage, and I told him my three stories.

" Ah," he said, " this is very curious—you should write it all down."

"Yes," I said, "I have it all in my mind, but I will write it all down."

He went on—"What made me think it especially curious is, that some few weeks ago I had a long talk with Gladstone myself in London.

I told him how sadly he had disappointed us. That we had looked to him to fight the battle of the Church in the House of Commons, irrespective of power and place, and he had not done it in any particular. I enumerated several.

He listened very patiently, and made me two very remarkable replies :—

1. *"My dear Bishop, What is the use of my talking about these things to* FIVE HUNDRED BRAHMINS *in the House of Commons?"*

2. *"All the points you have specified and others like them, are* INTUITIONS *to you, and men like you, who have sucked them in with their mother's milk. They are your foundation, that upon which you build."*

3. *"My case, let me say, is a different case. I was born and bred in an uninfluenced habit of life; and in my case every one of these things are the produce of the working of my own mind, simply."*

Here observe he clenched, by his own admission, what has been said about his order and habit of mind in this publication.

I am told that Bonamy Price, no mean judge of men, has said of Gladstone—*"you know he has not one intuition."*

In a letter from Lord Beaconsfield when he was Mr. Disraeli, he says—

"MY DEAR ARCHDEACON,—A fanatic* is a dangerous man, and when he is first Minister and leader of the House of

* Mr. Gladstone is "a fanatic" in respect of two things. (1) In respect of " the Great Liberal Party," and himself the Leader, once real, now nominal, of it. (2) In respect of his being " the only man who can govern England."

Commons, much more dangerous. It is true of Gladstone what Gerald Hamilton said of Burke, that his intellect is so profound, and his imagination so prolific, that he can, six times in every twenty-four hours, maintain that opposite truths are *the* truth, and the only truth."

Well, I wrote in reply. "I don't know that I could have put it as well as you have, but it is the conclusion at which I have arrived long ago from abundant evidence."

One evidence remains. Some five years ago I was sitting with a dear friend and his wife, a man highly honoured among us down here. He said to me, "Denison, you know more about Gladstone than anybody else." "Yes," I said, "I think I do."

"Well, tell me about him. He is a dear old friend and I used to go after him once. Gave that up long ago. But now I not only cannot go with him, but I cannot understand him a bit."

I said, poaching upon dear old Saunders, "I'll tell you all about Gladstone in a minute."

"*Gladstone has persuaded himself that he is the only man that can govern England.*"

He started in his chair. "What makes you start so?" I said. "Why it is curious. It is very little time ago that I put to Mrs. Gladstone the same question I have put to you, and she said, "*Oh, William knows he is the only man who can govern England.*"

"Well," I said, "you may be sure I did not get my inspiration from Mrs. Gladstone: but you see we are at one upon the point.

"Save that," Mrs. Gladstone says, "William *knows,*" as becomes a wife. I only said "*has persuaded himself,*" as becomes a looker-on.

This concluding story gives the key unlocking the casket containing the inner mind of the author of—

"The Church in connection with the State," 2 vols. 8vo. Murray, 1841.

"I am the only man who can govern England." How soon after 1841 that mind was made up I cannot say. But facts which have now to be stated appear to prove that the time cannot be very long.

In 1847, I published my first pamphlet: "A Letter to Mr. Gladstone upon the prospects before the Church of England in respect of her Parish Schools," arising out of the fact of the birth of the Committee of Council on Education, carried in 1839 by 2: in House of Commons, 725-273; * in House of Lords, for, 118; against, 229; majority against, 111.†

It will, I think, be found that in that letter I fore-shadowed in substance every principal step taken by the Committee and by Parliament—for the two things are by no means one and the same thing—down to 1870, when the apex was placed upon "the State" column reared against "the Church" by the device of "The Time Table Conscience Clause" of Mr. Forster's Bill.

This clause has deceived many: on the other hand, it has opened many eyes.

It does these things:

(a) It robs the Priest of the Parish of his Office in the Parish School.

(b) It turns *Education*—a Religious thing throughout in its only true nature and character—into an hour's, I think now it is a half-hour's, *instruction*, placing it on precisely the same level—in practice a *lower* level—with a lesson in arithmetic.

(c) It transcends the old "Conscience Clause"—more than transcends, it violates and destroys that which had

* I believe, but cannot verify at this moment, that Mr. Gladstone voted here in the Minority.

† For all details upon this subject I beg to refer to "Notes of my Life," Third Edition. Parker: Oxford and London. 1879.

all along been relied upon as the main lever for upheaving and overthrowing the Church School—the so-called original Conscience Clause. For the Bill creates *compulsory* schooling in all schools helped by State grant. A parent not sending his child to the schools is to be fined. The parent may say as much as he pleases that it is *against his religious conscience* to send his child to a school where the religion of the Church is not taught. The answer is, " You must send, or be fined." It is a stupendous mockery and most unblushing contradiction. But there it is. The parent's religious conscience has served its purpose, and is, as a worn-out tool, thrown away.

Liberal Policy is really an unclean and ghastly thing, even in the best hands that handle it.

This is a small digression—under my cirumstances it will, perhaps, be pardoned. And, indeed, it has a direct bearing upon my present subject, Mr. Gladstone's character and actions, for he was First Minister when the Bill became law.

I return now to my *catena*.

Mr. Gladstone replied to my letter, saying that in the main he agreed with me, but did not pledge himself for details.

He went on to direct my special attention to the danger of the "Management Clauses" just coming into life.

He wrote subsequently to say that the Archbishop of Canterbury had asked him to move a resolution at the Annual Meeting, and that he had declined upon two grounds. 1. That he was not satisfied with the attitude of the Bishops in the school matter. 2. That he was unwilling to be placed in a position as against me.

In 1852, when the schools of the Church had been sacrificed at the joint hands of Parliament, Committee of Council, and " The National Society for promoting the

Education of the Poor in the Principles of the Church "
—Mr. Gladstone joined a Government comprising those
who had been from the first principal agents in this
nefarious transaction.

Upon this I made my attempt to turn him out of
Oxford in 1853.

One day of the fifteen days' polling—the last fifteen
days polling in England—I was sitting in the Chair of
the Committee Room, when a letter was brought me
from Mr. Gladstone.

He wrote to say that my letter in *The Times* was doing
him harm without true cause, and that it was making
men suppose that I was quarrelling with him because he
had supported me in the School battle, and had now
deserted me.

That I knew that this was not so, for that, though he
had sympathized with me, he had not co-operated with
me.

And he asked me to write a letter to his Committee for
publication to this effect.

I replied the same hour, saying his account of his own
action was quite correct, and that I would so write.

But that I should have to add to my letter what he
appeared to have forgotten, viz., that it was his own
letter in 1847 which first flogged me up to fight the
school battle.

I sent my answer to his Committee. I remember that
they thought it wiser not to publish it in the interests
of their own cause.

In 1851 I was principally concerned in bringing the
men together who issued a Protest in the "Gorham
case."*

They assembled many days in the Vestry of S. Paul's,
Knightsbridge, by permission of Mr. Bennett, one of our

* Notes of My Life, pp. 198-9.

number. Our meetings were afterwards transferred to Mr. Gladstone's house in Carlton Gardens.

Mr. Gladstone was often present and concurred in the Resolutions passed.

But he was the only one of us who did not append his name to the Resolutions.

My last conversation with Mr. Gladstone was some four or five years ago, I forget which, when I was preparing for meetings in London, at Exeter Hall and St. James's Hall, and in many parts of the country for keeping the Prayer Book as it is. I asked him a question.

" Can anybody do a more unwise, almost mad, thing than the bringing of any Church matter before Parliament ? "

He said, " Nobody."

This is what I have for many years been trying to *insense* my dear friends in the Lower House of Convocation of Canterbury, but without success.

Now, Mr. Gladstone has contemplated since 1851 and 1854, to my certain knowledge, the matter, not of this or that detail of Church interests, but, of " dis-Establishment" coming before Parliament, and I understand him to say now that it is an " open question." Does he mean anything, or does he not mean anything ? We have at least the right to know this from the Author of " The Church in Connection with the State," 1841—" the only man who can govern England."

Mr. Gladstone, either as First Minister of the Crown or as Cabinet Minister, has become responsible for every one of the inroads made upon the constitutional position of the Church of England since 1832 ; among these Abolition of Church Rate, leaving it to Churchmen to maintain Church and Churchyard, not for themselves only, but for everybody else. Destruction of the Church school, leaving it without any real title to the name—Secularization of Universities—Alienation of Endowments bequeathed to help the poor scholar—with other like things. There is hardly anything remaining but " dis-Establishment."

We have then, I say, at least, the right to know what Mr. Gladstone has *made up his mind to* upon the whole matter; if it be possible for him to tell us.

If it is not possible, then all that is left us is to say, with Christopher Wordsworth, late Bishop of Lincoln, that as Mr. Gladstone has not, irrespective of place and power, defended and maintained the Church of England in years gone by, so he cannot be supposed to be ready to defend and maintain it now. Nay, that he has no reason to be surprised if he be regarded as the ostensible leader of the most dangerous adversaries of " Church and State."

SUMMARY.

Of all things that I have known in a long life, the history of Mr. Gladstone's career is the most melancholy and greatest warning to every statesman.

1. The man first, and for a time, in all the power of unblemished character and mighty intellect, Defender, Maintainer, Advocate, Improver of the use of the Gift of God to the People of England, the Gift of " Church and State."

2. The man dazzled with the vision of " Governing Power," turning away his eyes from his " first love," and wandering away into paths of man's " inventions."

3. The man content to surrender one after the other principal elements of " Church and State " to the popular cry.

4. The man become the Prince of the Opportunists.

5. The man first the Patron, then the follower,

then the agent of the " Red Radical." Paving the way in his company for the miserable deceits of Irreligion, Socialism, Communism.

6. The man who has not hesitated to apply Church Property to secular uses.

7. The man who votes for the " Deceased Wife's Sister " Marriage Bill; a thing in itself, and in its necessary adjuncts and followings, the breaking up, by Law of the Land, of all sanctity and purity of Marriage.

8. The man, who having written over the door of the House of Commons

" Civil and Irreligious Liberty "

has bound himself to set open the door, that any number of Bradlaughs, *presenting themselves to take the Oath*, may be ushered and welcomed in. For are they not an element of the great Liberal Party ?

9. The man who sacrificed Gordon to the disputes and difficulties of a discordant Cabinet of " the Great Liberal Party."

10. The man of no decisions except the one decision to govern England by the help of the great Liberal Party, however composed.

11. The man of many and mighty words but of obscurest meaning.

12. The man who has destroyed the substance, and left the shadow of the " Church School."

13. The man who has "set to his seal" upon the "Board School."

14. Finally,—and it is *the* key which unlocks the casket of a life,—the man, by his own confession, of "no intuitions." In their absence, the persuader of himself from day to day in an ever increasing ratio, by a process, hard to describe in words but, in his case, not difficult to understand, that the rule of State craft in every question, whether its title to consideration be Divine or human, is simply the rule of "practical politics."

15. The intellect his King. The conditions and circumstances of the day the guide to the conclusion of the day, ever shifting as the "exigencies" of the Governing Power may demand. Ending always at a lower point in the history of England's citizenship than that at which they stood the day, aye the hour, before.

Is there any *public* action wrongful in itself, injurious, in fact, or by tendencies, to the Divine Gift and Constitutional Position of the Church of England, which Mr. Gladstone, the author of "The Church in Connection with the State, 1841," has not supported as leader of "the Great Liberal Party"?

Is there any recognition or "magnifying" of that Position which has not suffered in his hands when weighed in the balance of " practical politics " ?

For there is such a thing as "*condemnare diminuendo.*" We have an Anglicism upon this practice which I forbear to cite. It is to be found in the preface to Pope's " Satires."

I am told that Mr. Gladstone has lately written something against reasoning by Syllogism.

How like the man who must have his *pros* and *cons* upon every conceivable subject of human thought ; Divine and human.

And, no doubt, reasoning by Syllogism is found to be, in some cases, very inconvenient.

Nevertheless, for myself, having still abiding in me respect and love for reasoning by Syllogism, I will conclude with a Syllogism, *e. g.*

The first and greatest thing to care for in English life is " the backbone of the Great Liberal Party."

" The Nonconformist is the backbone of the Great Liberal Party."

The first and greatest thing to care for in English life is " the Nonconformist."

What has become, 1841-1886, of all Mr. Gladstone's " Ayes " in Parliament, and out of it, *for* the Church of England, in the last forty-five years ?

'· The Noes have it."

People of England, look at the two Firms in the field and their stock in trade:—

I. "THE GREAT LIBERAL PARTY."—Messrs. Chamberlain and Dilke, Gladstone and Harcourt, Labouchere and Bradlaugh.

At home.—Secular instruction without Religion. The fruit, general Irreligion. No Church and Crown. *Robbing GOD. Unscrupulous trading upon crass ignorance of new Electors. Socialism, Communism, native and imported. Dismemberment of Empire.

Abroad. — Hesitation, Indecision, Truckling, Ignorance, Blundering, Reckless Waste of Public Money, Alienation, Contempt.

At home and abroad. —"Decline and Fall."

II. " THE CONSERVATIVE PARTY."—Messrs. Salisbury and Cabinet.

At home.—Care for the poor, who " shall never cease out of the land" (Deut. xv. 11). Religious teaching in Schools—*i.e.*, Christian Education. Church and Crown. Constitution of old England

* Psalm lxxvi. 4, 5.

—*i.e.*, " The Crown and the three Estates of the Realm." Rendering to GOD the things of GOD. All manner of legitimate improvement.

Abroad.—Dignity, Firmness, Knowledge, just and well-measured Economy, Respect, Confidence.

At home and abroad.—A Saved Empire, National Prosperity.

People of England,
look and choose
which you will deal with
of the two Firms.

EHEU! AMICI, AMICI:

SED MAGIS AMICA

VERITAS.

EAST BRENT, *December 11th*, 1885.

NOTES.

A. EVERY day brings nearer the prospect of another Election, with greater issues than even Irish dis-Memberment. The note of Irish dis-Memberment, with view of alluring to the succour of "the Great Liberal Party" the "Home Rule" vote, has already been sounded from Hawarden.

B (pp. 3, 36-8-9). When the prompting and guiding Counsellor of a man is himself, there being present to him no dominion of higher counsel than himself, and without appeal; then inevitably, and, in the case of the Baptized, by way of retribution, there is not found there the *Mens Conscia Recti.* In other words, there is no Rule of Right and Wrong without appeal for the mind to be conscious of. .

The man, thus left to himself and his own guiding— a guiding never able in itself, by necessity of human nature, to prevent his going astray, fills up the vacancy in thought and action with the *Mens Conscia opportunitatis*—that is, in the case *of the politician*—I do not say *of the Statesman*—with the sense of opportunity for dealing a blow upon an opponent, and making a step forward in some matter of worldly policy.

This tends irresistibly to accumulated exaltation of self, and of Intellect; as, after all, CHRIST's Gospel notwithstanding, the rightful king of the Christian life.

C. It would not be a clean and wholesome business to trace the authorship of the " Cow and Acre bribery and corruption " so largely employed, and with considerable success, by "the Great Liberal Party" in the late Election.

I know of nothing at once more wicked and more ridiculous.

Let us suppose the process of this *coup de terre* to have received its sanction by law, and its practical accomplishment.

Why the ink of the little transaction would hardly be dry—and I suppose my brethren of the law would take good care that there should be, at least, *some* ink— before re-accumulation of land into fewer hands would have begun—and, even supposing it not to have begun, what is to become, under infinitesimal division of land, what is to become of all improvements in the Science of Agriculture, and its better adaptation to the necessities of the English People, and the special circumstances of their case in respect of population and area, and application of means, hitherto not brought into general use, for making cultivation of the land of England really remunerative; and bearing its full part in providing for the sustenance of the People of England ?

For, as in all other Trades, so in the Trade Agricultural you require Capital.

But, under the conditions supposed, the Capital very rarely exists; and, so long as the subdivision remains, will very rarely be found in connection with it.

I think it much to be regretted that " Conservatives " at the late elections not uncommonly should have taken a leaf out of " the book of tricks," not to use here stronger language, however just, published and circulated by the adversary, and have said so much about sub-division of land being *in itself* a good thing.

It got muddled up somehow with making transfer of

land by sale easier and less expensive, and with ceasing
of power to entail. Things with which it has really
nothing to do. These may be wise things, the other is a
silliest thing. I do not feel at all sure myself even that
they may be wise things !

D. For the parent, again, compulsory school teaching
crushes out parental responsibility. The parent, almost
universally in the case of the working-classes, handing
over the child to the schoolmaster to be taught *no
religion.*

For the school teacher, this his function in respect of
the child reacts upon himself; and if he began with
some soundness in the Faith, he can hardly end with any.

> *Vires acquirit eundo.*
> *Facilis descensus.*

If any man desires to learn what is the *one only* way
in which it behoves a Christian man to deal with the
matter and manner of " Education," he will do well to
procure and read the Resolutions of the Roman Catholic
Bishops in England, and the Letter of Pope Leo XIII.
thereupon. London, December, 1885.

E. (p. 10, par. 1.) There is the Conservative Political
only ; and there is the Conservative Religious *and* Political: Religious, because *the* basis of his Conservatism is
the Church of England.

The Conservative, Political only, is a sound wholesome
citizen. More I cannot say for him.

Again, there is the Conservative Religious, but fearful ;
and there is the Conservative Religious, and not fearful.

The first knows, but does not do. The second knows
and does.

If we are compelled by the position to choose between
" the Great Liberal Party " and " the Conservative

Party," the choice is a very simple matter. But we should all be more comfortable if the element of fear was purged out of the Conservative Religious.

For "the Great Liberal Party," it has no perception—being morally blind in this, as in a great many other things—of what is meant by "the Service of GOD being perfect Freedom."*

F. There is the Jesuit Ecclesiastical, and the Jesuit Political.

The Jesuit Ecclesiastical is content to stop at nothing for Ecclesiastical Power's sake.

The Jesuit Political is content to stop at nothing for Political Power's sake.

ADDENDUM.

AT the close of the earliest copies of "Mr. Gladstone" I had inserted three well-known words from Horace to denote the contrarious and over-powering absurdity of Mr. Gladstone's posing as a " Churchman," but, for love of that " Great Liberal Party " which has long become his first love, acting and even speaking publicly as a " Nonconformist."

But I saw that "the Liberal man"—who would not only rob me and mine of " such things as we have," but even, if he could, of the sense of the ridiculous—might, in his despair, try to make some poor capital of the adaptation; and I took the words out.

* 2nd Collect. Morning Prayer.

CONDENSED SUMMARY OF CHARGES AGAINST MR. GLADSTONE.

I sum up in a few words my indictment against Mr. Gladstone. If there be any answer to it—which I do not believe there is—let us have it *ambagibus remotis, prœvaricatione, circumlocutione.* My indictment is,—That, in the absence of anything in him to *control,* or even to *moderate,* the despotism of intellect, and consequent self-reliance upon every question, divine as human, ecclesiastical as civil, he has become a slave to himself, to his own position and lust for governing power; to the universal application, and never-ending mystifications and delusions from day to day of what he calls " practical politics."

I delayed purposely publication of my pamphlet till the Elections were over. The indictment it contains wants deeper consideration than can be given in the hurry and confusion of meetings and canvassings. I submit it now to the calmer thoughts of some less excitement.

January 14th, 1886.

POSTSCRIPT.

A.

I received, January 2nd, the additional evidence to the peculiarity of Mr. Gladstone's mind in early childhood at his only school before Eton, contained in the following letter. It fills up very curiously the only space in the record which I had not been able to fill up myself.

DEAR MR. ARCHDEACON,

I have just seen and read your " Gladstone," and take the liberty of sending you the *opinion* of the Rev. W. Rawson, late Vicar of Seaforth, under whom Mr. Gladstone received his only education before he went to Eton.

I had the pleasure of spending a few days at Seaforth Vicarage in 1872, not long before Mr. Rawson's death ; and this is what he told me of Gladstone. Speaking of Gladstone, he said, " *From the day he entered my house until the day he left, aye, and until this day, I have never been able to tell whether he is sane or insane.*"

Your statement of Gladstone having no intuitive perception is also corroborated by another expression used by Mr. Rawson, that " *Gladstone could never originate an idea of his own.*" " *He always shone best in carrying out other people's ideas.*"

And certainly the ideas he has attempted to carry out are step by step on the descending scale.

The only question before one while he lives is, what next ? and next ? •

From such dangerous demi-*gods*, good Lord deliver us. Thanks for your Pamphlet.

Faithfully yours,

Since Mr. Gladstone came back to office by a side wind ; trimming, as " an old Parliamentary hand," his boat too craftily for his opponents "in Church and State"; too craftily for their plain and trusting honesty ; and effecting a permanent coalition between the " Red Liberal," " the Socialist," and " the Communist ;" I have been searching history, ancient and modern, for a parallel.

I can only find one.

It is the frequent action of the Chorus in a Greek Tragedy. A foul murder is proposed. In the Chorus case, a human murder, commonly of a near relation. In Mr. Gladstone's case, a murder Civil and Ecclesiastical. The "relation" here also not remote. Chorus begins by remonstrating warmly, in finest and most touching language, to most beautiful music.

But finding no response to remonstrance ; and that the exercise of virtue is not "practical;" it goes over to the murderer in virtue of its permanent position as chief adviser ; encourages, aids and abets him in committing the murder at the earliest practicable "opportunity ;" urges this upon him in the like finest and most pathetic language ; to the same beautiful music ; as being the "practical politics" of that particular day.

B.

How exactly has Lord Palmerston's forecast of Mr. Gladstone, which I *know* to have come from Lord Palmerston's mouth, been now fulfilled.

" *Did you meet that fellow as you came upstairs ?*" " *I met Gladstone just outside your door.*" " *That's the fellow I mean. He'll destroy everything we have got left.*"

Lord Palmerston was the Tory Prime Minister of the

then Liberals. He could not have been in power without them, and they could not have been on " right hand" of the Speaker's Chair without him. There have been other like "arrangements" of late years. Some call them "compacts ;" or " conspiracies ;" or " treaties offensive."

But the " arrangement" of 1886 throws them all into the shade.

Mr. Gladstone has been claimed as of all Parties, one after the other. "Everything by turns, and nothing long." But he has never been anything but " Gladstone;" always *going downstairs,* as he did from Lord Palmerston's room, hoping to find something *at the bottom ;* with his own all-governing hand always to guide it farther down still.

G. A. D.